JURASSIC PARK III™

Movie Storybook

A storybook adapted by
Marc Cerasini

Based on a motion picture screenplay written by
Peter Buchman

Based on the characters created by
Michael Crichton

Random House 🏠 New York

Special thanks to:
Cindy Chang & Dawn Ahrens of Universal Studios
and
Barbara Ritchie &
Randy Nellis of DreamWorks
and to
Alice Alfonsi, Jason Zamajtuk,
Fred Pagan, Jonathan Ellis,
Lisa Findlay, Artie Bennett, Christopher Shea,
Jenny Golub, Colleen Fellingham, and Stephanie
Finnegan of Random House
for their work on this book.

www.randomhouse.com/kids

Library of Congress Catalog Card Number: 00-111483

ISBN: 0-375-81288-1

Printed in the United States of America
June 2001

10 9 8 7 6 5 4 3 2 1

JURASSIC UPDATE

By our science reporter

Ever wonder what happened to Jurassic Park?

It's been over eight years now since billionaire John Hammond first began his ambitious project to bring dinosaurs back to life.

Employing an army of genetic scientists, Hammond used prehistoric DNA to clone an array of dinosaurs and other ancient species.

According to Hammond, he had planned to open his private dinosaur preserve—located on two islands off the coast of Costa Rica— to paying tourists.

Unfortunately, a number of deadly accidents (not to mention a few *very* expensive lawsuits— one stemming from a lawyer being eaten by a T. rex!) convinced Hammond and his InGen Bio-Engineering corporation to abandon the idea.

Eventually, the world learned of this secret project. Who can forget that stunning news footage of a live T. rex roaring through the streets of San Diego four years ago?

These days, scientists around the world continue to express their desire to study in Jurassic Park. Sadly, the United Nations and Costa Rican authorities continue to keep the park off-limits to all humans. Calling the area extremely hazardous, they have continued to maintain the no-boating, no-flying zone around both Isla Sorna and Isla Nublar.

But is *that* the end of the story?

Not likely! Despite the restrictions, daredevils are periodically risking their very lives just to get a glimpse of the now world-famous Jurassic Park. . . .

Isla Sorna
120 miles west of Costa Rica

"There it is!" called Eric Kirby, pointing to the rocky shoreline of the tropical island.

Beside him on the deck of the small speedboat, Ben Hildebrand raised his video camera and pushed the record button. "Dinosaurs, here we come!" he said with a smile.

Ben was a friend of Eric's mother. He had arranged this dream trip for the thirteen-year-old, and Eric still wondered how the man had done it. No boats or planes were allowed anywhere near Jurassic Park's islands. But that didn't matter to Ben, or to the skipper of this little private tour boat.

"Are you ready to go?" Ben asked.

Eric nodded. He'd been ready since the first day he'd heard of Jurassic Park!

"Get us as close as you can," Ben told the skipper.

"Not too close," the man replied. "You don't want them to eat you!"

Moments later, the two-person parasail opened, and Eric and Ben were lifted off the deck. Rising up over the water, Eric scanned the jungle, ready for a glimpse of a real live dinosaur. Everything was peaceful for a while, but then a violent jolt startled him. Eric looked down and saw that the skipper was gone!

"Something got to him!" Ben cried. "The boat's out of control. Unclip your line!" As Eric and Ben drifted helplessly toward Isla Sorna, a pair of cold, predatory eyes watched . . . and waited.

eeks later, in a suburban backyard, Dr. Alan Grant watched with amusement as two tiny dinosaurs battled each other.

"Rrrrrowww! Grrrrrrrr!"

After a few minutes, Dr. Grant spoke to the little boy playing in the sandbox. "Actually, Charlie, those two are herbivores. They wouldn't be interested in fighting each other."

Dr. Grant picked up two other toy dinosaurs. "See, these are carnivores," the paleontologist explained. "And this one here—see its claws—this one here uses its claws to gouge the throat of its opponent."

Charlie's eyes grew wide.

"Uh, Alan," said Charlie's mother, Ellie Satler, "he's three. Why don't you wait till he's five?"

"Oh, right," Dr. Grant replied.

He smiled at little Charlie and made the toys dance on the sandbox edge. "*Happy* dinosaurs!"

Charlie giggled. He liked the dinosaur man.

A car turned into the driveway.

"That must be Mark," Ellie said, running to greet her husband.

Dr. Grant rose, and the two men shook hands.

"Daddy! Daddy!" Charlie cried. "This one is a her-ba-bore."

Over dinner in Mark and Ellie's dining room, Dr. Grant talked about his recent work.

"We have a new site in Montana," he said. "Well, at least we do until the money runs out. I'm on a fund-raising tour to raise cash for the excavation."

"Did you find anything interesting?" Ellie asked.

"Raptors mostly. Your favorite," Dr. Grant teased.

Years ago, Dr. Grant had worked closely with Ellie. Then the two of them had nearly been killed during a visit to Jurassic Park—by raptors. They'd both escaped, but afterward they'd gone their separate ways.

"Raptors lived and hunted in packs," Dr. Grant reminded Ellie, "and I have a theory that they communicated through the sounds they made. That's how they worked together as a team."

Ellie was excited about Dr. Grant's theory, but her husband, Mark, was unimpressed.

"What do you do, Mark?" Dr. Grant asked.

"International relations, mostly," Ellie's husband replied. "Treaty law. Boring stuff."

After dinner, it was time for Dr. Grant to leave.

"Let me know if I can help," Ellie told him as they said good-bye. "If you need me for anything, just call."

The next day, Dr. Grant spoke at a local university. After his talk was over, he faced some tough questions.

"What's the point of digging up bones?" one student asked.

"Yeah," echoed another. "Once the United Nations decides how to handle Isla Sorna, scientists can go to the island and look at live dinosaurs for themselves."

A reporter rose and asked, "Isn't paleontology itself in danger of extinction?"

"No," Dr. Grant replied impatiently. "Paleontologists study dinosaurs. The *real* dinosaurs lived sixty-five million years ago. What's left of them is fossilized in stone. What InGen created are theme park monsters, nothing more."

The reporter seemed puzzled. "You're saying you wouldn't want to study them if you had the chance? You wouldn't want to go back?"

Dr. Grant shook his head. "No force on earth or heaven could get me back to Jurassic Park."

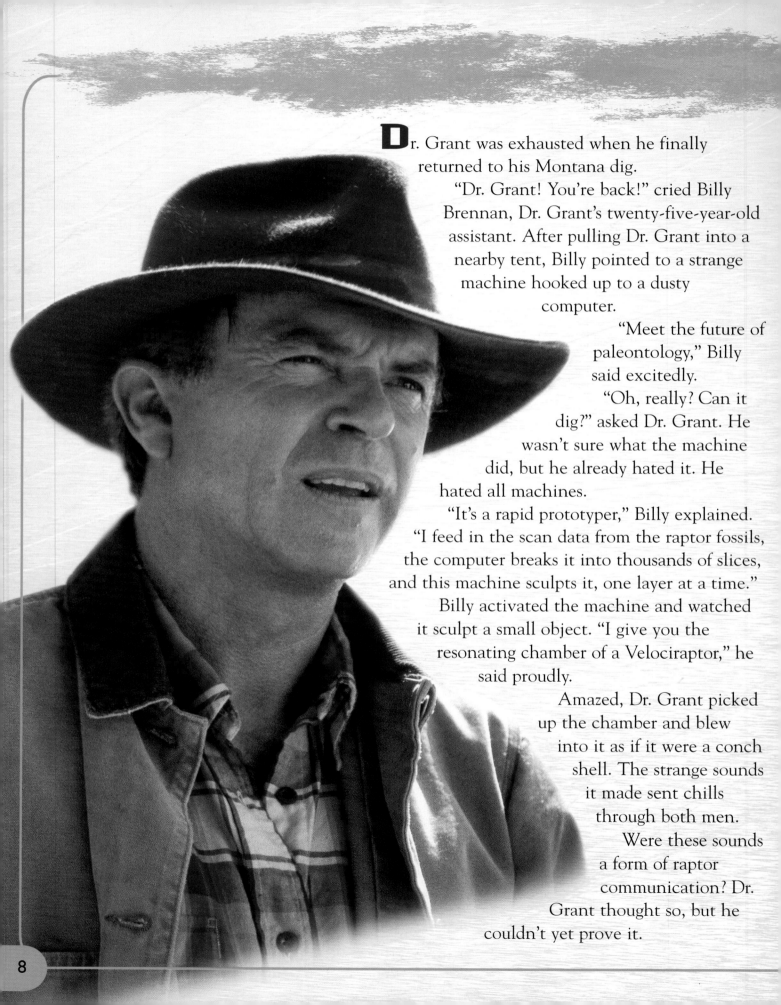

Dr. Grant was exhausted when he finally returned to his Montana dig.

"Dr. Grant! You're back!" cried Billy Brennan, Dr. Grant's twenty-five-year-old assistant. After pulling Dr. Grant into a nearby tent, Billy pointed to a strange machine hooked up to a dusty computer.

"Meet the future of paleontology," Billy said excitedly.

"Oh, really? Can it dig?" asked Dr. Grant. He wasn't sure what the machine did, but he already hated it. He hated all machines.

"It's a rapid prototyper," Billy explained. "I feed in the scan data from the raptor fossils, the computer breaks it into thousands of slices, and this machine sculpts it, one layer at a time." Billy activated the machine and watched it sculpt a small object. "I give you the resonating chamber of a Velociraptor," he said proudly.

Amazed, Dr. Grant picked up the chamber and blew into it as if it were a conch shell. The strange sounds it made sent chills through both men. Were these sounds a form of raptor communication? Dr. Grant thought so, but he couldn't yet prove it.

"You must be Dr. Grant," said a man who had suddenly appeared at the opening of the tent. A woman stood beside him. "My name is Paul Kirby, and this is my wife, Amanda."

Dr. Grant frowned. He had no time for strangers.

"I have an interesting proposition for you," Paul said with a smile.

At dinner that night, Paul and his wife told Dr. Grant about their plans.

"We hired a private airplane to take us flying over Isla Sorna, and we want you to be our guide," he explained.

Dr. Grant shook his head. "I have already taken that little adventure tour. Once was enough. Besides, I understand the islands are in a no-flying, no-boating zone."

"We've gotten special authorization to fly over it," Amanda said. "Please come. You don't know how important this trip is to us."

"If you go, I would be prepared to make a big donation to your work," Paul said, waving his checkbook. "A really *big* donation."

Billy stared at the checkbook, then at his teacher. They badly needed money for their research. *C'mon, Dr. Grant! Billy's eyes seemed to shout. Don't say no!*

A few days later, Dr. Grant was sitting inside a small plane with Billy next to him.

As they approached Isla Sorna, a radio signal crackled through the pilot's headphones. "Unidentified airplane! You are in restricted airspace. Redirect at once."

Nash, the pilot, ignored the message and flew on. His copilot, Udesky, switched the radio off. Nash banked the airplane and dived lower. Everyone was staring out the windows at the island below.

"Look there!" Dr. Grant cried. "An Apatosaurus!"

Billy was thrilled to see a living dinosaur. "I'm used to bones. It's weird to see skin."

Suddenly, Dr. Grant heard an odd sound.

"Is that the landing gear?" he asked.

Dr. Grant stared at Paul and Amanda Kirby. They refused to meet his gaze.

"You can't land!" Dr. Grant protested. "It's too dangerous!"

Dr. Grant rushed forward to the cockpit. But halfway there, the steward, Cooper, grabbed him.

"This plane cannot land!" Dr. Grant shouted. But Cooper's fists swung hard, and Dr. Grant's world faded to black.

When Dr. Grant opened his eyes again, he heard Amanda Kirby's voice from outside the plane. "Eric," she called, "are you there? Answer me!"

Who's Eric? wondered Dr. Grant. He and Billy stumbled out of the plane and saw that they had landed on a weed-covered runway. Paul Kirby stood near the plane, watching Amanda pace, while Udesky, Nash, and Cooper walked into the jungle.

"Where are those three going?" Dr. Grant asked Paul.

"They're setting up a perimeter," Paul replied. "Making it safe for us."

Dr. Grant shook his head. "On this island, there is no such thing as safe."

Grrrrrrrraaaaaaah!

"What was that?" Paul whispered.

Suddenly, Nash and Udesky came running out of the jungle. There was no sign of Cooper. "We've got to go!" Udesky cried.

A second earsplitting roar rocked the jungle. The creature was closer now.

Everyone ran for the plane. Nash started the engines, and Udesky rushed to the cockpit.

Billy tried to stop him. "What about the other guy?"

From the jungle came Cooper's terrified scream.

"We're going!" Udesky shouted.

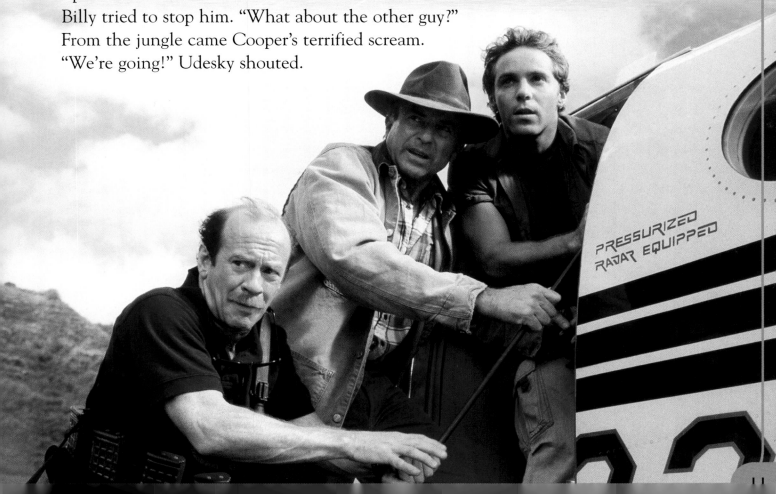

PRESSURIZED
RADAR EQUIPPED

From her seat inside the small plane, Amanda saw the creature at last.

"Oh, my goodness!" she cried as a gigantic Spinosaurus lumbered out of the jungle. It was huge—almost fifty feet long and sixteen feet high with a tall, bony sail along its spine.

Cooper was running from it, waving at the plane to stop. But the man didn't have a chance. The creature bent low and snapped its toothy jaws around him.

Then the Spinosaurus stepped in front of the oncoming plane. Nash pulled back on the stick, trying to soar over the creature. But one of the propellers clipped the beast's armored back and the airplane plunged into the jungle, crashing into the thick branches of a tall tree.

Inside, the passengers were dazed but alive.

Nash tried the cockpit radio, but it didn't work. "Who's got the satellite phone?" he cried.

Paul tossed the phone to Nash, but all Nash got was a busy signal.

Udesky opened the door, then froze. The plane was so high in the treetops there was no way for them to get down!

Suddenly, Amanda began to scream. A gigantic eye glared at them through the cockpit window. The Spinosaurus had followed them!

With an ear-shattering roar, it ripped away the nose of the plane!

Udesky and Nash gasped as the Spinosaurus stuck its long snout inside the cockpit. The two men lunged for the passenger compartment.

Udesky made it. Nash didn't.

The dinosaur's jaws closed on Nash's leg. Within seconds, he was dragged away.

In no time, the Spinosaurus came back for another course of its meal. Ramming its long snout inside the aircraft again, it tried to grab Amanda with its giant teeth. She pulled her legs back in the nick of time, and the knife-like teeth snapped shut on empty air. As everyone rushed toward the back of the passenger compartment, the plane began to tip over. In a shower of leaves and broken branches, the wreckage crashed to the ground at the Spinosaurus's feet.

The dinosaur kicked the airplane, and the twisted metal hull skidded across the jungle clearing. The passengers tumbled like clothes in a dryer.

The Spinosaurus caught up to the plane again and crushed the metal hull with its gigantic foot. Then its giant jaws began to rip the remains of the plane apart.

"This way!" Dr. Grant cried.

He and the others crawled through a jagged rip in the side of the plane and ran into the jungle.

Sensing movement, the Spinosaurus turned. When it spotted the escaping prey, it chased after the humans.

With Dr. Grant in the lead, the group darted among the trees. The Spinosaurus was close on their heels, but the deeper into the jungle they ran, the thicker the tree trunks became. Soon the thick trees were so close together that the huge creature could no longer squeeze between them!

The humans ran in panic until they couldn't run anymore. When they could no longer hear the roar of the Spinosaurus, they stopped in a clearing to catch their breath.

Gasping, Amanda looked up. Then she screamed. The humans had stumbled upon a Tyrannosaurus rex!

"Nobody move a muscle," Dr. Grant whispered. It was a full-grown bull Tyrannosaurus, and Dr. Grant hoped the creature wouldn't notice them if they stood perfectly still.

The rex's eyes scanned the area for a long moment, but the predator failed to react. Dr. Grant was relieved. The rex didn't see them!

Then, just when the predator was turning away, Udesky panicked. Breaking from their group, he began to run. He didn't get far before the rex spotted him, roared, and began to chase him.

Now everyone else had to run, too!

They ran through the trees at top speed, right back in the direction of—

"Oh, no," said Dr. Grant on an exhaled breath.

A shadow rose in front of them. It was the Spinosaurus! Paul grabbed Amanda's hand and dragged her behind a tree. Udesky and Billy jumped into the bushes. Dr. Grant tried to flee, too, but couldn't. His foot was trapped in the twisted roots that covered the forest floor!

He closed his eyes in fear. But the rex and the Spinosaurus didn't even notice the tiny human.

The two huge predators began to circle each other. The rex roared so loudly that it hurt Dr. Grant's ears. The Spinosaurus shook the tall, bony sail on its back and snarled. Finally, Dr. Grant broke loose and dived

between two stout tree trunks.

With a low growl, the rex struck the other predator with its tail. The Spinosaurus howled with rage, then leaped at the throat of the yelping rex.

The humans watched in both horror and awe as the Spinosaurus tore at its enemy. As the battle raged, Dr. Grant crawled toward the others.

"We've got to go!" he told them.

Earthshaking roars pierced the jungle as the two predators continued their fight, and the humans vanished among the trees.

"Why did you bring us here?" Dr. Grant demanded when they found a safe spot.

"Our son, Eric, is on this island," Amanda said. She told them how her friend Ben had taken Eric parasailing near the island and never come back.

Dr. Grant saw a look of sadness on the woman's face. "How many days has Eric been missing?" he asked.

"Eight weeks," she said.

"Eight weeks," repeated Dr. Grant, shaking his head. "And do you really think your boy is safe?"

"He's smart. And he knows a lot about dinosaurs," Amanda said with determination.

Dr. Grant sighed. "I'm sorry, but we can't help. We have to get off this island as soon as possible. It's just too dangerous."

Paul put his arm around his wife. "We're not leaving without our son," he said.

Dr. Grant nodded. "You can stick with us or you can look for him. Either way, you're probably not getting out of here alive."

"What do we do?" Paul asked Udesky as Dr. Grant and Billy headed off.

"I think we should start searching for your son," answered Udesky, "in the direction Dr. Grant is going."

The five survivors returned to the wreckage of the plane to search for food and equipment. Paul and Amanda changed cloths.

Udesky found a rifle, but it was bent.

Billy found his camera and began taking pictures of the Spinosaurus footprints.

"How would you classify that creature?" Dr. Grant asked, pointing to the tracks.

Billy shrugged. "Obviously a super-predator. Maybe a Suchomimus?"

"They never got that big," Dr. Grant said.

"Then I give up," Billy said.

"It's a Spinosaurus aegypticus," Dr. Grant informed his student.

Billy turned to Paul. "I don't suppose that check you wrote us is any good?" he asked.

"No," Paul replied.

"There's no Kirby Enterprises, is there?" guessed Dr. Grant.

"I own a place called Kirby Paint and Tile Plus in Enid, Oklahoma," said Paul. "And if we make it off this island with my son, I swear I'll make good on the money. Even if it takes me the rest of my life."

As a roar rose from the jungle, Udesky added: "However long *that* is."

As they headed for the coast, Amanda called her son's name over and over again.

"Quiet!" Paul told his wife. "Dr. Grant says this is dangerous territory."

"Who cares?" Amanda cried. "Dr. Grant isn't looking for our son!"

"Hey, look!" Billy said, pointing to a parasail dangling from a tree. Paul checked the gear.

"It's Eric's! He's here," Paul said excitedly. Then he spotted something in the weeds.

"That's Ben's camera," Amanda cried.

The video camera still worked, so Paul played back the tape. On the recording, they saw Eric and Ben land. Eric was safe, but Ben was hurt and stuck in the tree. Eric was climbing up the tree to help Ben when the tape ran out.

"Eric is fine," Paul said with a sigh.

But then Billy tugged the parasail out of the tree, and Amanda screamed!

A man-size skeleton was tangled in the branches. It had been hidden behind the parasail.

"It's Ben!" Amanda sobbed, recognizing his clothes.

As Billy rolled up the parasail and stuffed it into his backpack, Amanda began to cry. "He's alone out there. Our baby is all alone."

"Don't worry," Paul said. "We'll find him."

"Dr. Grant! Look here!" Udesky called.

Udesky was staring at a hole in the ground. Inside were lots of eggs.

"Raptors," Dr. Grant said grimly.

"What's a raptor?" Paul asked.

"A predatory dinosaur. If we see one, we might live," Dr. Grant told them.

"That's good!" Paul said in relief.

"But you never find just *one*," Dr. Grant added. "Raptors hunt in packs."

The group moved on, but after a few minutes, Amanda realized someone was missing.

"Where's Billy?" she asked Dr. Grant.

"Billy!" Dr. Grant shouted. "BILLY!"

Billy ran up to them, camera in hand. "I got some great pictures of the nest. This proves raptors raised their young in colonies. We could write a paper!"

Dr. Grant grunted with anger. Losing Billy, even for a moment, had really shaken him. "Let's go," he said.

After a long trek through the jungle, they found InGen's abandoned laboratory. The buildings were falling apart and rusty cars were scattered around the compound.

"I'll bet Eric is here," Paul said.

Soon they found an area filled with computers and huge incubators. Tubes and wires hung everywhere. Half-formed creatures floated inside glass tanks.

"This is how you make dinosaurs?" Amanda asked.

"This is how you play God," Dr. Grant answered with disapproval.

While Billy took pictures, the others looked around. Amanda was surprised to find a full-grown raptor head inside one of the glass tanks. As she leaned in for a closer look, the head moved!

Suddenly, a hungry raptor darted out from behind the machinery. The dinosaur tried to bite Amanda, but its huge head got caught between two tanks.

"Get out!" Dr. Grant cried as the raptor tipped the tanks over and then began to chase them.

The humans ran out of the building. They could hear the raptor crying for help. Other raptor voices began howling in reply. The noise came from all around them.

"Head for the trees!" Dr. Grant cried.

The humans rushed through the parking lot toward the jungle.

All of a sudden, a pack of hungry raptors charged forward. Hoping to evade them, Dr. Grant led the others into the middle of a hadrosaur herd, which was munching grass near the jungle's edge. But the predators ignored the plant-eaters. For some reason, the raptors only wanted the humans!

As everyone scattered, Dr. Grant saw Billy trip over a root and drop his camera bag. Dr. Grant snatched it up.

"Keep going!" he called to Billy.

A pack of raptors cut off Dr. Grant. He climbed a tree and watched them gather below. The raptors barked and padded in circles around the tree.

Dr. Grant knew the creatures were talking to each other. But what were they *saying*? And how was he going to escape?

Suddenly, he saw a metal canister bounce into the clearing. With a hiss, it began to spew smelly smoke. The raptors barked and ran away, their eyes stinging from the oily fog.

Then Dr. Grant saw a shape outlined in the smoke. A *human* shape!

"This way!" a boy's voice called. "Hurry!"

The smoke stung Dr. Grant's eyes, and he could not make out his rescuer's features. So he just followed where the boy led. Eventually, they came to a tanker truck buried up to its headlights in a swamp.

Dr. Grant climbed into the truck and found himself in a small space lit by a battery-powered lamp.

"Are you Eric Kirby?" Dr. Grant asked the boy.

Eric nodded.

Dr. Grant watched the thirteen-year-old seal the hatch. Eric was no longer an ordinary boy. There was something wild and primitive about him. The kid had certainly learned how to be a survivor.

"Your parents are here," Dr. Grant told him.

"My parents?" Eric asked. "On *this* island?"

"Yes," said Dr. Grant. "They're looking for you."

Eric's shoulders slumped. "They'll never make it. They can't even manage when the cable goes out."

Dr. Grant smiled. "You'd be surprised what people can do when they have to."

"You're Dr. Alan Grant," Eric said, recognizing the man from his book photos. "What are you doing here?"

"Your parents . . . they, uh . . . *invited* me to come with them to look for you."

"I read your books," Eric said. "The first is the best. You liked dinosaurs back then."

"Back then, dinosaurs hadn't tried to eat me."

Dr. Grant looked around. There were lamps, a pair of binoculars, and lots of candy wrappers. Eric had been living on chocolate for weeks.

"When InGen cleared out, they left a lot of stuff behind," the boy explained.

"Any weapons?" asked Dr. Grant.

"No," Eric replied. "And I just used the last of the gas grenades."

"I'm astonished you've lasted eight weeks," Dr. Grant told the boy.

Eric looked stunned. "Is that all it's been? I thought it was longer."

Then the boy handed Dr. Grant a candy bar, and they settled in for the night.

At dawn, Eric and Dr. Grant crawled out of their hiding place. "How much of this island have you explored?" Dr. Grant asked.

"I stayed pretty close to the compound," said Eric.

"Well, I say we head for the coast," said Dr. Grant. "We'll keep an eye out for your parents and my assistant as we go. It's the best plan."

Sometime later, Dr. Grant and Eric came upon a valley. An old barge was moored alongside the bank of a river far below.

"It looks to be in good shape," Dr. Grant said. "We could follow the river out to the ocean, where the Coast Guard will find us."

"Then we go home?" Eric whispered.

"Then we go home," said Dr. Grant.

Suddenly, they heard an unexpected sound—the melodic ringing of a cell phone!

"That's my dad's telephone!" Eric cried.

"How do you know?" Dr. Grant asked.

Eric smiled and sang the Kirby Paint and Tile Plus commercial's jingle to the music of the phone. Then he began to yell: "Dad! Dad!"

Not far away, Billy and the others heard Eric's voice.

"That's Eric!" cried Paul.

He and Amanda raced through the jungle until they were stopped by a metal fence with rusty spikes along the top. On the other side, they saw Dr. Grant and Eric.

"Sweetheart!" Amanda cried. "You're okay!" She hugged her boy through the fence.

Billy was relieved to see Dr. Grant alive, and happy to see he had the camera bag, too.

"How did you know we were so close?" Paul Kirby asked.

"I heard your phone ring," Eric replied. "And that stupid jingle from the store."

Paul was surprised. "My phone? I don't have it. I loaned it to Nash back at the airplane. He must have had it when that big dinosaur—"

Before Paul could say another word, the humans heard a low growl. . . .

At the edge of the forest, the Spinosaurus stood staring at them. The ringing was coming from the creature's belly.

Then the Spinosaurus roared, and Dr. Grant realized that the creature was on *his* side of the fence!

"Run!" he yelled.

Eric and Dr. Grant took off with the Spinosaurus crashing through the trees on their heels. On the other side of the fence, Paul, Amanda, and Billy ran alongside them.

As they ran, Dr. Grant spotted a hole in the fence. "Through there!" he cried.

Eric jumped through the gap with Dr. Grant right behind him. The Spinosaurus snapped its jaws shut, barely missing Dr. Grant's legs.

The Spinosaurus ripped its way through the rusty fence, then stomped over the wreckage after its fleeing prey.

Dr. Grant saw a concrete building ahead. It had stout walls and was perched on the side of a steep canyon. He led the group through its doorway. Then the humans slammed the heavy metal door and bolted it. They could hear the Spinosaurus howling in rage as it tried to break through. The bolts strained, but held.

When they were safe, Billy approached his teacher. "Sorry, Dr. Grant. I could've gotten you killed. What did you do with them?"

Dr. Grant was puzzled. "With what?"

"In my bag," Billy said nervously.

Dr. Grant opened the camera bag and stared at its contents—two raptor eggs.

"I just thought if we could get a raptor back to the mainland, we could study it," Billy explained. "We could get enough money to fund our digging for ten years—"

Dr. Grant shook his head angrily, unable to believe what he'd just heard.

"You have to understand," continued Billy, "I did it with the best of intentions."

"Some of the worst things imaginable have been done with the best of intentions," snapped Dr. Grant. "You rushed in with no thought to the consequences. You're no better than the people who built Jurassic Park."

"What do you think this place is?" Paul asked, interrupting them. There were huge windows overlooking the canyon on one side of the building.

"Some kind of observatory," Dr. Grant said.

"There's a boat at the bottom of the canyon," Eric added. "We can use it."

In the room was a spiral staircase that led down into the canyon. Dr. Grant climbed down. The others followed.

Dr. Grant stopped on a landing and held the camera bag over the edge of the canyon. He was ready to smash the eggs on the ground far below, but Paul stopped him.

"Keep them with you," he said. "If you've got something the other fellow wants, you don't throw it away. Those raptors may want us dead, but they want these eggs more. That's the only advantage we've got."

Dr. Grant knew that Paul was right. He placed the camera bag in his backpack.

Through a break in the mist below, Dr. Grant spotted the river at the base of the canyon. But when he stepped off the landing and onto the next set of rusting steps, the staircase suddenly broke free and tumbled down the canyon wall!

Paul pulled Dr. Grant back to the landing just in time.

After catching his breath, Dr. Grant looked around. "How about if we try *that* way?" he asked, pointing to a covered catwalk that spanned the canyon like a narrow bridge. The far end of the catwalk was invisible in the mist—but it was their last hope.

Amanda was nervous. "Do you think it goes all the way across?"

Dr. Grant shrugged. "Only one way to find out."

Dr. Grant stepped onto the catwalk and felt it sway back and forth.

"It's not that strong. We'd better cross one at a time," he told the others.

When he reached a sturdy landing halfway across the canyon, he stepped off the catwalk to rest. He couldn't see the others through the mist, so he called out to them, "Come on over! One at a time."

A few minutes later, Amanda arrived at his side.

"Come on, Eric!" she called to her son.

Eric slowly walked into the thick fog. The narrow structure swayed under his feet. He couldn't see very far in any direction.

Halfway across, Eric heard a loud thump. A dark shape appeared through the haze. Something else was on the catwalk with him.

"Mom?" Eric called softly.

On the catwalk's landing, Dr. Grant was studying the steel mesh net around them. The net was gigantic, covering the entire canyon like a cage.

But why would InGen want to build a canyon-sized cage? Dr. Grant wondered.

Suddenly, he gasped.

"What is it?" Amanda asked.

"This is a *bird*cage!" Dr. Grant cried.

From somewhere in the fog, Eric screamed. Hearing his son's screams, Paul charged onto the catwalk. But it was too late. A Pteranodon had already snatched Eric up in its claws and was flying off with him!

Eric struggled in the creature's grip, but it did no good.

"Eric!" cried Paul in horror. He watched helplessly as his son was carried away.

The Pteranodon dumped Eric into its nest. He landed on a pile of bones. Instantly, six baby Pteranodons lunged at him, beaks snapping.

Eric snatched a skull from the pile of bones and swung it wildly, determined to fend off the hungry babies as long as he could.

Dr. Grant was shocked to see Billy climbing back up to the observation deck. He looked ready to jump.

"Billy! No!" Dr. Grant shouted.

"I know the consequences!" Billy replied.

Then he jumped. He dropped a long way; then a chute opened above him like a colorful umbrella. It was the parasail they had found in the jungle!

"Eric! Hold on!" Billy cried.

As Billy swooped over the nest, Eric jumped up and caught his leg. The boy was lifted over the heads of the snapping Pteranodons.

Suddenly, the mother dived out of the sky with an angry shriek. Her beak ripped a hole through the parasail. Billy and Eric spun in the air.

"Let go!" Billy cried.

Eric plunged into the cold river. When he came up again, he was gasping for air.

Billy and the crippled parasail slammed into the side of the cliff. His harness caught on a spire of rock. Billy watched helplessly as a flock of Pteranodons circled above him.

Meanwhile, Dr. Grant, Paul, and Amanda were trapped on the crumbling catwalk with an angry Pteranodon. There was nowhere to go but down.

The three humans tumbled into the river. They hit the water hard and swam for shore.

Billy was still trapped on the cliff. A Pteranodon swooped low, coming in for an attack. Its beak cut the harness, and Billy plunged into the river. But as he waded to shore, the whole flock of Pteranodons swarmed him.

"Billy!" screamed Dr. Grant.

"It's no use," Paul said, seeing more Pteranodons heading their way.

He pulled Dr. Grant toward the double-gated fence that Amanda and Eric had already raced through. As the gate was shut, the angry Pteranodons shrieked and cawed in rage, battering the gate with their bodies.

The humans moved on, unaware that the rusty lock on the gate was beginning to weaken. . . .

A full moon rose in the sky as the barge chugged downriver. On deck, the humans heard a familiar jingle. The satellite phone was ringing!

"Quiet!" Dr. Grant whispered, sure that the Spinosaurus was close by.

They spotted large brown mounds on the flat shore. Spinosaurus dung! The ringing sound was coming from one of those piles.

Everyone rushed ashore. They held their breath as they dug into the smelly mounds.

"I've got it!" Amanda cried, pulling the telephone out of the stinky mess. It was still ringing! She activated the phone.

"Vacation in Mexico," a recorded voice said. "You can enjoy a meal in one of our fabulous restaurants or . . ."

She shut off the phone to save power.

Suddenly, a hungry Carnotaurus stomped out of the jungle. The creature took one sniff of the dung-covered humans and lumbered away. Not even a dinosaur would eat something that smelled as bad as they did!

"I can't help but be a little offended," Paul said.

As night fell, the humans cleaned the satellite phone and tested it. The battery light was flashing. There was not much power left.

"Don't call the United States embassy," Paul said. "They won't do a thing."

"We have to call someone we can count on to help us," said Dr. Grant.

Eric noticed movement under the surface of the water. He pointed it out to Dr. Grant. Just then, a fish leaped out of the water. Then another.

"Something scared them," said Eric.

Dr. Grant looked at Paul. "Get the motor started," he said urgently.

Climbing to the top of the wheelhouse for better reception, Dr. Grant dialed the phone.

Back in America, little Charlie answered.

"Hewwo?"

"It's the dinosaur man! Get your mommy!"

"It's the dinosaur man," Charlie said.

But all Ellie Satler heard was a dial tone. *What did Dr. Grant want?* she wondered, and punched *69 to find out.

The Spinosaurus rose from the water and slammed into the barge. Dr. Grant stumbled and dropped the phone. He jumped off the wheelhouse seconds before the creature tore the structure away.

The Kirbys took cover inside the rusty cage on the deck. Dr. Grant jumped in, too. Then the barge began to sink—with the humans inside the cage!

The phone rang. Dr. Grant reached through the bars to grab it off the deck.

"Ellie!" he cried. "Can you hear me?"

Ellie heard Dr. Grant, then the unmistakable roar of a live dinosaur!

"Site B!" Dr. Grant screamed. "The river—"

Then the line went dead.

"**W**e should keep moving," Dr. Grant said gently.

"NO!" Eric howled. "We can't leave Dad."

Amanda steadied her son.

"Let me tell you a few things about your dad," she said. "He's very clever, very brave, and he loves you very, very much."

Eric wiped away a tear. "He loves you, too."

"He loves *us*," Amanda continued. "And I know that your dad would want to know that we're safe."

"You should listen to your mother," a voice said from out of the darkness.

Paul, half-drowned, stepped out of the shadows. Eric rushed to his father and hugged him.

So did Amanda.

At sunrise, they began moving again. As they walked along a narrow path, Eric caught up with Dr. Grant.

"That lady you called. How do you know she can help us?"

"She's the one person I can always count on," Dr. Grant replied. "She's saved my skin more times than she realizes."

A noise from far away reached their ears.

"Did you hear that?" Dr. Grant asked.

Eric nodded with excitement. "It's the ocean!"

The group rushed forward, bursting into a clearing. Above them, the sun was bright and the sky cloudless. But suddenly, a dark shadow fell over them. All that separated them from the ocean was twenty yards of sand—and a dozen raptors!

Warily, the creatures circled the humans. To everyone's surprise, the raptors did not attack.

"They want the eggs," Dr. Grant said. "Otherwise we'd be dead already."

Cautiously, Dr. Grant eased the backpack off his shoulders. A female raptor stomped forward, eyeing him.

"Everyone get down," Dr. Grant whispered. "She's challenging us."

The humans dropped to their knees. The female raptor walked over to Amanda.

"She thinks I stole the eggs!" Amanda gasped. "Give me the eggs," she whispered to Dr. Grant.

Cautiously, Dr. Grant reached into his backpack and pulled out the camera bag. As he did, his fingers brushed against something he'd put in there days ago—the sculpted model of a raptor's resonating chamber!

He slowly pulled it out, put it to his lips, and blew, trying to re-create the same eerie pitch he'd heard the raptors make. It was their cry for help.

The raptors barked, but did not attack. Then they made the same eerie sound in reply! Dr. Grant's theory was correct. He was communicating with raptors!

Suddenly, the raptors tilted their heads as they heard a new sound. The humans strained their ears, but did not recognize the noise until a moment later.

Helicopters!

Working quickly, Amanda took the eggs from Dr. Grant and placed them on the sand.

The female moved closer. She picked up an egg. The male raptor came forward and grabbed the second one. Then the creatures took off, vanishing into the jungle.

Dr. Grant and the Kirbys quickly got up and hurried over a low hill. A man in a business suit stood on the beach, a bullhorn in his hand.

"Dr. Grant?" the man asked.

Dr. Grant halted in his tracks. So did Paul, Amanda, and Eric. They were stunned by what they saw.

Dozens of U.S. Navy warships plowed through the waves off the coast of Isla Sorna. Military helicopters hovered in the air while others idled on the beach. A squad of United States Marines fanned out along the beach in a defensive perimeter, weapons ready.

"Wow!" Eric cried.

They had been rescued!

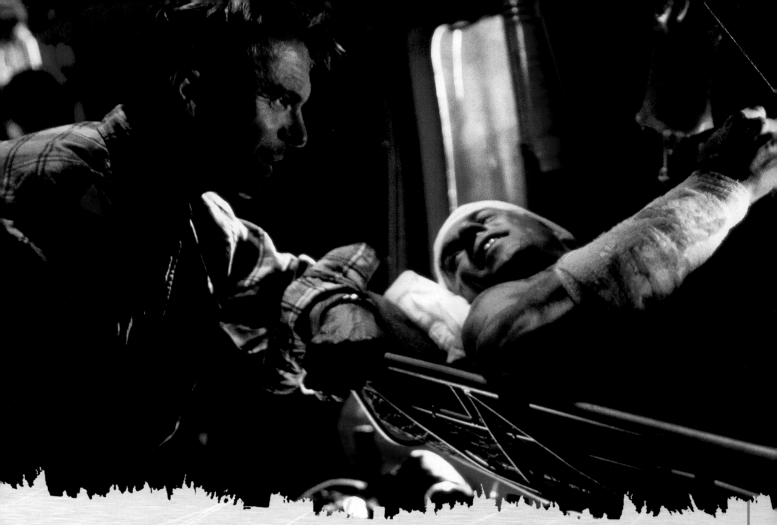

As they climbed aboard a Marine Corps helicopter, Dr. Grant saw a young man lying on a stretcher.

There were bandages on his arms, and the top of his head was covered by gauze. He was hurt, but he was alive.

"Billy!" Dr. Grant cried, stunned. "You're okay!"

Billy smiled. Then he gestured to the battered fedora on the floor next to the stretcher. "I rescued your hat," he said.

"Well, that's the important thing, isn't it?" teased Dr. Grant.

"He lost a lot of blood," the medic said as Billy closed his eyes, "but he'll be fine."

Relieved, Dr. Grant sat down and strapped in as the helicopter took off. As they flew away from the island, the pilot pointed.

"Hostile at nine o'clock!" he cried as Pteranodons surrounded the aircraft. A Marine grabbed his rifle, but Dr. Grant stopped him.

"They're just flying in formation," he explained. "They think we're one of them."

Eric watched the creatures. "Where do you think they're going?" he asked.

"To find a nesting ground," Dr. Grant replied. "It's a whole new world for them."

"As long as they don't nest in Enid, Oklahoma, that's fine with me," Amanda said. Then she turned to her husband. "Let's go home, Paul."

The copilot handed a radio headset to Dr. Grant. "It's for you."

It was Ellie. "Are you okay?" she asked.

Dr. Grant smiled. "Yes. I'm fine."

"Thank goodness!"

He heard the relief in her voice. Then she said, "Alan, I thought you never wanted to go back to Jurassic Park. You said there was nothing for you to learn there."

"I did say that, didn't I?"

"So what were you doing?" she asked.

Dr. Grant watched the Pteranodons as they flew toward the rising sun of a new day.

"Evolving," he replied.